To Rowan, Fabio, Matteo and Nia — AF

To my sister, Kate — EF

STRIPES PUBLISHING
An imprint of Little Tiger Press
1 The Coda Centre, 189 Munster Road,
London SW6 6AW

A paperback original
First published in Great Britain in 2016

Text copyright © Adam Frost, 2016
Illustrations copyright © Emily Fox, 2016
Back cover images courtesy of www.shutterstock.com

ISBN: 978-1-84715-678-5

A CIP catalogue record for this book is available
from the British Library.

Printed and bound in the UK.

10 9 8 7 6 5 4 3 2 1

Fox Investigates

A Taste for Adventure

ADAM FROST
ILLUSTRATED BY EMILY FOX

Stripes

IT'S SHOWTIME!

Wily Fox, the great detective, was standing in front of a large TV studio. The neon lights of Tokyo flashed above and behind him. A long queue of animals clutching sleeping bags snaked along the pavement. Wily walked past them and approached the main entrance.

"Get to the back of the queue," barked a security guard, a large rhino holding a big stick.

"I'm here to see Charlie Cheetah," said Wily.

"Nice try," said the rhino. "But the boss

doesn't have time for visitors, and nobody jumps the queue while I'm on duty. If you want to be in the audience for the *Megachef* final next week, you'll have to get to the back."

"But I don't," protested Wily.

"Course you do," said the rhino. "Everyone does. *Megachef* is a worldwide phenomenon."

Wily pulled out a letter. "I'm a worldwide phenomenon, too. And Charlie Cheetah has asked to see me."

The security guard studied the letter. "Seems genuine," he grunted, looking Wily up and down. He took out a badge. It was in the shape of a frying pan and marked MEGACHEF GUEST. He pinned the badge to Wily's lapel and whispered, "Today's password is *prawn crackers.*"

"Prawn crackers," Wily said to the rhino security guard outside Charlie Cheetah's office.

"You're free to pass," said the security guard, opening the door wide.

"Ah, Mr Fox," said Charlie Cheetah, coming out from behind his desk. "Thank you so much for coming." He bowed at Wily, who bowed back, then gestured towards a large leather chair.

"Please sit, Mr Fox. Would you like some mocha ice cream?" asked Charlie. "Or perhaps some *amanatto* – they're like doughnuts."

"No, thanks – I've just eaten," said Wily.

"You don't mind if I do?" asked Charlie, opening a desk drawer.

"Not at all," said Wily.

"Great!" Charlie took out a large doughnut. In between mouthfuls, he told his story. "I've always loved food, Mr Fox *(chew, swallow)*. Even as a child *(mmm, delicious)*, when my friends were out playing football, I was still inside *(BURP, excuse me)*, taking hours over my lunch."

"I can imagine," said Wily.

Charlie started on another doughnut.

"Five years ago, I started working for Tokyo TV as a newsreader *(hiccup, oh dear)*. But they were looking for ideas for new shows *(chomp, gulp)*. I proposed *Megachef,* with me as producer, writer and presenter. They let me make one episode, to see if people liked it. Fifty million people watched it in Japan alone."

"Wow," said Wily.

Charlie started on a large cup of tea.

"Now it's the biggest show in Asia *(slurp)*. Amateur chefs compete from every country in the continent. They're all desperate to be crowned *(glug) Megachef* champion."

Charlie dabbed his lips with a huge napkin.

"The final is in three days' time," he said. "The problem is – someone is trying to sabotage it."

"Sabotage?" said Wily. "What do you mean?"

Charlie pressed a button on his desk and a screen slid down on the opposite wall.

"Watch this," he said, pulling out a tray of cakes. "It's from the *Megachef* semi-final two nights ago. We were down to three contestants and one was about to be knocked out. Everything rested on this last cooking challenge."

The screen came to life and Wily saw three contestants standing in front of a long worktop. On the left, there was a nervous-looking shrew wearing thick glasses. In the middle, there was a confident-looking lemur in a baseball cap. On the right, there was a gloomy-looking coyote with bags under her eyes.

"He's Shoma Shrew," said Charlie, between mouthfuls, "he's Lenny Lemur and she's Kia Coyote."

It was the dessert round. Shoma Shrew was making a meringue, Lenny Lemur was tackling a trifle and Kia Coyote was starting a soufflé. Charlie fast-forwarded to the end of the show.

Charlie himself appeared on screen. "And now let's bring on the judges to find out which of our three semi-finalists will NOT be back for the final next week!"

A horse wearing a monocle came on the set, followed by a frowning platypus.

"Haruki Horse is Japan's greatest chef," Charlie explained to Wily. "Petra Platypus is a famous Australian food critic. Now, look at this."

"Let's start with Kia Coyote," said the Charlie on screen.

Haruki Horse, Petra Platypus and Charlie all tasted Kia's soufflé.

"Delicious," said Haruki and Petra – and Charlie agreed.

Then they tried Lenny Lemur's trifle.

"Amazing," said Petra and Haruki – and Charlie agreed.

Finally they tried Shoma Shrew's meringue.

"Completely incredible," said Haruki.

"Absolutely sensational," said Petra.

The Charlie on screen looked horrified as he tasted the meringue, but he quickly stammered, "Yes. Er, good. Very good."

Charlie paused the recording. Then he pulled a meringue from a fridge under his desk.

"This is the meringue that Shoma made. Taste it."

Wily put a spoonful on his tongue and winced.

"Exactly," said Charlie. "I don't know if he used too little egg white or added too much sugar, but it's revolting. So, Mr Fox, I need you to find out why my judges awarded maximum points to THIS."

"Did you ask them after the show?"

"Yes, they both looked at me like I was mad. I made them taste it again and they insisted it was delicious."

"Odd," said Wily.

"They've sent Lenny Lemur home, and Shoma and Kia have gone through to the final. Lenny was a real audience favourite as well.

It's like they're trying to destroy the show. What if they sabotage the final, too?"

"Have you done anything to upset them?" asked Wily.

"No," said Charlie. "They've been with the show since the beginning. I thought we were ... friends. Then they do this! Thankfully no one in the audience noticed anything out of the ordinary. But the press have been asking questions. One food critic noticed that the meringue looked unusual. If something like this happens in the final, they'll say the show is rigged. It'll all be over. My life's work ruined."

"Then I need to start investigating at once," said Wily. "The most obvious place to start is with the remaining contestants. Where are they staying?"

"The Tokyo Lodge Hotel," said Charlie.

"OK," said Wily. "Time to pay them a visit."

WILY CHECKS IN

The hotel was a five-minute walk away, which gave Wily time to phone his trusty assistant, Albert Mole. Whenever Wily needed a gadget, a contraption or just some information, Albert was always on hand to help him.

"Albert, are you in Tokyo yet?" asked Wily.

"Yes, I've set up a temporary HQ underneath the Hamarikyu Gardens," said Albert. "What did Charlie Cheetah want?"

Wily explained the case to Albert and then said, "Now I need you to get me information on the pair who made it to the final – Shoma Shrew and Kia Coyote. And find out if anyone had a grudge against the contestant who got knocked out – Lenny Lemur."

Wily stopped talking, pressed a button on the side of the phone that transformed it into a rubber stun Frisbee and flung it over his shoulder.

Someone had been following him.

When he turned round, whoever had been there was already gone. Wily spotted a shadow moving down a side alley and heard echoing footsteps. He grabbed the Frisbee-phone from where it had landed and raced down the alley, but it was too late. There was no one in sight.

Wily crouched down, looking for paw prints.

He saw a small smudge in a patch of mud, possibly made by a rodent's back foot. Gerbil? Mouse? Or maybe ... shrew? Could Shoma Shrew be trying to stop his investigations?

Wily arrived at the Tokyo Lodge Hotel. It was decorated in a traditional Japanese style, with sliding paper walls, wooden floors and hanging lanterns everywhere. As he walked into the lobby, Wily was hit by a wave of noise. Lenny Lemur was halfway through a press conference. Journalists were fighting to photograph him and ask him questions. Next to Lenny stood a fierce-looking lemur wearing a large turban. Wily guessed this was Lenny's mother.

"Are you disappointed to be going home?" asked one of the journalists.

"Yes, very much so," Lenny began.

"Of all the ridiculous questions!" his mother huffed. "Of course he's disappointed – he should be in the final! He's a fabulous cook."

"Will you compete again next year?" another journalist asked.

"I'll have to think about—" Lenny began.

"Of course he will!" his mother interrupted.

"He's a Kobe Lemur! We're the oldest lemur clan in Japan! Do you think we'll give up just because some half-witted horse and a pea-brained platypus made a stupid decision?"

"Mr Lemur," said another journalist, "the audience loved you. Have you got plans to—"

"Of course they loved him," Lenny's mother burst out. "He was the best chef in the competition. It's a scandal! It's an outrage! If I ever meet that Charlie Cheetah, I'll knock the spots off him!"

"Calm down, Mother," said Lenny.

"Don't tell me to calm down," she replied. "That shrew and coyote can't cook – it's as simple as that! I could smell that terrible meringue from the front row. To lose to a pair of chumps like them is the worst thing of all!"

Wily glanced across to the left and saw the "pair of chumps" that Lenny's mother was referring to, waiting to be interviewed.

Shoma Shrew was wiping his glasses nervously on his sleeve. Had he run to the hotel after following Wily?

Kia Coyote was staring at her feet, looking slightly embarrassed by Mrs Lemur's insults. Was she feeling guilty because she knew the result was rigged?

"One thing's for sure," Wily said to himself. "If Lenny's mother finds out they're involved, she'll pull their heads off."

Then he had another thought. As Shoma and Kia were down in the lobby, he could look for clues in their rooms. He moved away from the journalists and approached the reception desk.

"Any mail for Room 13?" he asked.

The moose behind the desk moved away from his computer and turned to look at the pigeonholes. While he was doing this, Wily swivelled the computer screen round and quickly found the room list. Shoma – Room 8. Kia – Room 11.

By the time the moose had turned back to the desk, there was no one there.

Wily was at the end of a long corridor. On both sides of him were paper walls on sliding panels. He could see shadows through the walls – a polar bear talking on the phone, a skunk hunched over a laptop, a pelican watching TV in bed. Wily walked down the corridor and reached Room 8. There was no noise or movement inside.

Wily tried the door – locked. He pulled out a universal keycard that Albert had made for him during the Case of the Imprisoned Piglet and slipped it into the slot beneath the door handle. The light on the handle turned green.

Inside the room, Wily found nothing suspicious. Shoma's clothes were ordinary-looking and there were no unusual items tucked in the pockets or hidden in the sleeves. He opened a large suitcase at the end of the shrew's bed, but it just contained cookbooks, bottles of sauce and Shoma's lucky frying pan. Wily opened a bottle of ketchup and sniffed. It was just ketchup.

Then he heard a **PING** coming from Shoma's laptop. Wily went over to the desk and read:

> Shoma, my angel.
> You've brought us so much honour. You have reached further in life than anyone in our humble family has ever managed before. Try to keep your nerves under control. You can do it!
> Mum

Wily hesitated before clicking on Shoma's other emails – after all, the shrew was only a suspect, not a criminal. But Wily only had three days to solve this case – he had to be ruthless.

As he read, he quickly realized that Shoma's family was extremely poor. It seemed unlikely that he could have paid the judges. He also seemed very timid – not the kind of animal to use bribery or blackmail.

Time to explore Kia's room, thought Wily.

In Kia's room, nothing seemed out of the ordinary, either. As Wily was rummaging through one of the coyote's drawers, Albert called.

"I've run a thorough background search on the contestants," he said. "Lenny Lemur is most likely to have bribed the judges. His family is very wealthy. But he was knocked *out.*"

"What about Shoma and Kia?" asked Wily.

"They seem to be honest animals," said Albert. "Though there is one strange thing."

"What?" asked Wily.

"I managed to hack into the PSSST archives – got a five-minute window before they booted me out. Turns out PSSST has a file on both Kia and Shoma."

PSSST was the Police Spy, Sleuth and Snoop Taskforce. The head of PSSST, a bulldog called Julius Hound, often clashed with Wily over their methods of investigation.

"Why would PSSST have a file on them if they've never broken the law?" asked Wily.

"It is strange, isn't it," said Albert. "PSSST only keeps a file on animals that have a direct link to crime. And here's the strangest thing of all."

"What?"

"Both files are marked open," Albert said. "The investigations are ongoing."

At that moment, Wily heard a creaking noise behind him. He ended the call with Albert and turned round. There was a dark outline on the paper wall behind him. Someone was standing outside Kia's room. He didn't know how long they'd been there, but he guessed they'd been listening in to his conversation.

Wily didn't move.

Then there was a CRUNCH! and a RIP! and a ROAR! as the eavesdropper jumped through the paper wall, right at Wily.

Wily saw nothing but a muzzle and a large paw. He rolled sideways, trying to throw the attacker off, but the animal clung on to him. Struggling against each other, they tore through another paper wall, where two herons looked up from a game of chess, then another, and soon they were back in the hotel corridor.

Wily finally got himself on top. He pinned down his attacker's arms and drew back to get a proper look.

"Hello, Julius," said Wily. "Albert and I were just talking about you."

Julius Hound kept struggling. "Get off my case," he growled. "And get off me, too!"

"Not until you tell me why PSSST is interested in a cooking show," said Wily.

"What cooking show?" Julius snarled. "What are you talking about?"

"You're investigating Shoma Shrew and Kia Coyote," said Wily.

"We're investigating *everyone* in this hotel," said Julius. "Our suspect was seen here yesterday."

"What suspect?" asked Wily.

"Can't tell you," said Julius.

"Then I can't release you," said Wily.

Julius growled. "OK. We're on the trail of a ninja assassin. Last month she tried to assassinate the vice-president of Papua New Guinea. We've tracked her to Tokyo, but we don't know what she's doing here."

Wily released Julius and they both stood up.

"I'm on a completely different case, so you don't need to worry," Wily said. "I've been hired by Charlie Cheetah, the host of *Megachef.*"

Julius sniggered. "*Megachef?* You mean

that silly cooking show my wife watches? What are you investigating?" He grinned. "An undercooked sausage? A stolen tea cosy?"

"It doesn't matter," Wily replied. "But now you can stop following me. I assume it was one of your agents tailing me earlier on."

Julius looked genuinely surprised. "Not this time. I didn't know you were here till I saw you downstairs. You must have other enemies – besides me." He stomped off down the corridor. "And stay away from my ninja assassin," he barked over his shoulder.

Wily looked at the walls, now full of holes and flapping shreds of paper.

"We certainly tore through this place," he said.

RISE OF THE MACHINES

Wily was at Albert's HQ, studying a map of Tokyo.

"Did you know this city has 13 million people in it – twice as many as London?" Wily said.

"1.62 times as many – to be exact," called Albert from behind a large purple curtain.

"That gives me twice as many suspects," said Wily. "So there's no time to waste. The contestants seem honest enough. Now, what about the judges?"

"I thought you were going to say that," said

Albert, emerging from behind the curtain with a screwdriver in his hand. "That's why I've made you this." He pulled the curtain to one side to reveal his latest invention.

"A plank of wood?" said Wily.

"Jump on it," instructed Albert, smiling proudly.

Wily moved over to the striped board that stood on a bench in the middle of the floor. He jumped on to it. A blue light flickered under his feet. A gentle female voice said, "Footprint match. Wily Fox. Turbo surfboard activated."

A fin appeared on each side and a rocket sprang out of the back.

"Haruki Horse runs a restaurant in Kobe," said Albert. "That's about an hour away by plane. But on this surfboard, you can be there even faster. Tap the red disc with your heel to start. Tap again to stop."

"Cool!" Wily exclaimed. "Anything else I need to know about Haruki Horse before I go?"

"He's barely seen in public. Apart from when he's filming *Megachef*, he never leaves his restaurant. To get close to him, you'll need to use your cunning, your intelligence and *this spoon*."

Albert handed Wily a spoon with a row of flashing buttons along its edge.

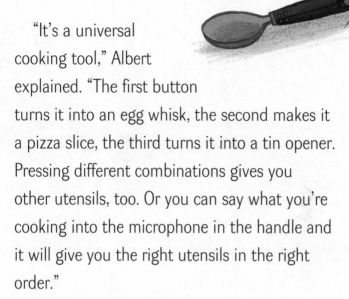

"It's a universal cooking tool," Albert explained. "The first button turns it into an egg whisk, the second makes it a pizza slice, the third turns it into a tin opener. Pressing different combinations gives you other utensils, too. Or you can say what you're cooking into the microphone in the handle and it will give you the right utensils in the right order."

Wily pressed buttons and watched the spoon grind and click into dozens of different tools.

"I thought you could apply for a job in Haruki's restaurant," said Albert. "As a world-class chef."

"Excellent idea," said Wily, putting the spoon in his pocket and picking up the surfboard. "Are you coming, too?"

Albert sighed. "Only if you promise to surf responsibly."

"I swear on my brother's life," said Wily.

Ten minutes later, Wily was riding a gigantic wave along the east coast of Japan, while Albert clung on to Wily's back with his eyes tightly shut. When the wave broke, Wily activated the rocket booster and zipped through the sky, landing on another gigantic wave.

"You swore on your brother's life you'd be sensible!" shouted Albert.

"I don't have a brother!" Wily shouted back.

Shortly after, they landed on the sand at Suma Beach Park, not far from Haruki's restaurant.

"So," said Wily, "this judge said that Shoma Shrew's meringue was delicious when it tasted revolting. Let's find out why."

"Please don't talk about food," said Albert, holding his stomach and collapsing on the beach in a heap.

Wily left Albert to recover and dragged his surfboard further up the beach. He leaned it against a rock and then walked along to the restaurant. Inside, it was very busy. Every table was packed with diners chatting, eating and ordering food.

You don't get to be a Megachef *judge unless you're a good chef,* thought Wily, *so why would he be risking his reputation by rigging the competition?*

His thoughts were interrupted by a large robot, which grabbed him by the collar and twisted him round to face the beach.

"EYEBALL SCANNED," it said.

"BOOKING NOT RECOGNIZED. YOU HAVE FIVE SECONDS TO VACATE THE PREMISES."

"Get your hands off me, you hunk of junk!" Wily exclaimed.

"HOSTILITY DETECTED," said the robot. **"INTRUDER WILL BE EJECTED."**

The robot whirred round to the side of the restaurant and kicked Wily into a giant dustbin.

"Well, this stinks," said Wily, climbing out of the bin. Then, looking up, he noticed a door marked STAFF. Remembering Albert's plan to pose as a chef, he brushed a mouldy grape off his shoulder and knocked on the door. Another robot appeared in the doorway. It looked very similar to the one that had just thrown him into the trash.

"Hello," said Wily, "I'm Etienne Pamplemousse, the most exciting young chef in France. I'd like to work for Haruki Horse."

"NOT POSSIBLE," said the robot.

"No vacancies?"

"EVEN IF YOU DID NOT SMELL OF MOULDY GRAPES," said the robot, **"MR HORSE NO LONGER HIRES ANIMALS. HE HAS REPLACED ALL HIS CHEFS AND WAITERS WITH THE LATEST T-PLUS-3 SERIES OF DOMESTIC ROBOTS."**

Wily glanced over the robot's shoulder into the kitchen and saw dozens of robots chopping vegetables, preparing meals and carrying plates.

"Impressive," Wily said. "You know, I should get myself a T-Plus-3. How much would a model like you cost?"

"MY RETAIL PRICE IS 10,000 US DOLLARS."

"What a bargain!" Wily said. "And, tell me, when did Mr Horse activate you?"

"I BEGAN SERVING MR HORSE SIX DAYS AGO. YOU HAVE FIVE SECONDS TO LEAVE THE PREMISES."

"I'm going, I'm going," said Wily. He wandered back round to the front of the restaurant, looking for Albert.

"Where have you been?" Wily asked when he found his assistant. "Sunbathing?"

"No, I've found a cave in the rocks," said Albert. "I'm setting up a new HQ."

"Listen," said Wily. "I think I can prove that Haruki was bribed."

"How?"

"Six days ago, he replaced all his staff with expensive robots," Wily explained. "It would have cost him over a hundred thousand dollars. That's serious money!"

"He could have earned it fair and square," said Albert. "He is quite famous. And Charlie Cheetah must pay him a fair bit."

"It's possible," said Wily, "but something smells wrong to me. I think someone gave him that cash."

"So what are you going to do?"

"I'm going to break into Haruki's office," said Wily, "and find out whether he's involved."

"But you just said his restaurant is staffed by robots," said Albert. "How are you going to get past them?"

"That's why I need your help," said Wily. "Here's the plan…"

Five minutes later they were standing outside Haruki's restaurant. Albert was wearing overalls and holding a toolbox.

As they approached the doors of the restaurant, the first robot whirred out again.

"We heard you have a problem with a faulty robot," said Wily.

"WHICH ROBOT?"

"Well … in fact … you," said Wily.

Albert pulled out a small black stick and zapped the robot with a strong electric current.

The robot crackled and slumped forwards.

Wily peered into the restaurant and then said, "Great, nobody noticed. Now, get going – quick."

Albert flipped open the control panel on the robot's chest and started fiddling with wires.

As he did so, Wily noticed that all the robot waiters had stopped what they were doing and were staring at them through the restaurant windows.

"Uh-oh, they know something's up," said Wily. "They must all be connected."

"I'll need two more minutes," said Albert, frantically snipping and twisting wires.

Two of the robot waiters were trundling towards the door. A red light was flashing on each of their chests.

"OK, I'll distract them," said Wily. He walked into the restaurant and rummaged around in his inside pocket where he always kept his disguises. He found a pair of large glasses and put them on. Then he said loudly, "I had a meal here last week and I left my hat behind."

A couple of the diners looked up.

Both robots stopped. The red lights on their chests flashed amber.

"NO HAT IN LOST PROPERTY," said one of the robots.

"Maybe it's over here," said Wily, walking towards a pot plant and knocking it over. "Silly me," he added.

"ACCIDENT IN LOCATION 7," said the second robot and went to clean up the soil.

"Actually, I was sitting over here," said Wily. He stumbled over a large vase, which smashed on the floor.

"BREAKAGE IN LOCATION 9," said the first robot, whirring over to the vase.

"Or maybe it was over here by the window," said Wily. He knocked a whole table to the floor, sending food and cutlery flying. "Sorry – I'm very short-sighted," he said.

"You nincompoop!" exclaimed a moose as he wiped soup off his antlers.

The two robots started to pick up the plates. A third and fourth robot steamed out of the kitchen and headed straight for Wily.

Wily quickly dropped down on to all fours.

"Is that my hat there?" he said, crawling through the robot's legs and heading to the kitchen.

But at the kitchen door, a fifth robot grabbed Wily and turned him upside down. The robot wheeled back to the entrance and threw Wily as far as it could. He landed with a splash in the sea. As he clambered back on to the shore, he saw Albert walking towards him.

"Please tell me we're in," said Wily.

Albert grinned. "We're in."

THE MYSTERY CALLER

Wily was sitting in the cave where Albert had set up their HQ. He was halfway through a video call with Charlie Cheetah.

"I knew that horse was involved," said Charlie, taking a bite of pizza heaped with twenty different toppings. "He's always been driven by money. Sadly his restaurant doesn't make enough to fund his lifestyle. That's why he became a *Megachef* judge – for the money. And he gets to do spin-offs. Recipe books, pasta sauce, cooking DVDs. Clearly these weren't enough." He gave an ear-splitting belch that made Albert's laptop shake. "But I still don't understand…" he said, starting on another pizza slice.

"What?" asked Wily.

"Why did Petra Platypus also say the meringue was delicious?" said Charlie. "Did someone get to her, too?"

"It's possible," said Wily. "Tonight I'm going to break into the restaurant and hopefully we'll find out who's been bribing BOTH Haruki and Petra."

"Good, good," said Charlie. He coughed and the screen was suddenly covered in tomato and melted cheese. He wiped a little hole in it and said, "Bye for now."

"That cheetah is one hell of an eater," said Albert in wonder.

It was midnight and Wily was standing outside Haruki's restaurant again. All the lights were off and the only sound he could hear was the lapping of waves on the beach.

Wily knocked on the glass door of the restaurant and, a few seconds later, a robot appeared and unlocked the door. It scanned Wily's right eye.

"YOU ARE RECOGNIZED AS A FRIEND," said the robot. **"YOU HAVE ACCESS TO ALL AREAS."**

"Much obliged," said Wily and strode in. "Where are the other robots?"

"ALL OTHER ROBOTS PLACED IN SLEEP MODE," said the robot.

"Well done, Albert," Wily said to himself. Then out loud he said, "Let's go to Haruki's office."

They came to a door at the back of the restaurant. The robot placed its hand over a sensor and the door hissed open. They went along a corridor and reached a second door. The robot punched a series of numbers and letters into a panel on the wall. The door opened and the robot wheeled into a small dark office.

"WAIT HERE," said the robot. "YOU DO NOT SHARE HARUKI'S DNA. SEVERAL ALARMS WILL BE ACTIVATED."

Wily watched as the robot wheeled into the office. A strange yellow gas started fizzing out of the floorboards but the robot said the word "wasabi" and it stopped. An arrow whizzed out of a hole in the wall, but the robot caught it and snapped it in two. A heavy metal weight dropped down from the ceiling, but the robot caught it and placed it on the floor.

"ROOM NOW SAFE," said the robot.

Wily stepped inside and a trap door appeared by his feet. He managed to fling himself sideways just as it opened, grabbing on to the edge of the pit with his left hand and then swinging himself up and over – back on to the floor.

"I thought you said the room was safe," said Wily.

"THAT IS THE WAY TO HARUKI'S OFFICE," said the robot.

Wily looked into the hole. A ladder led down into a small bunker.

"Wow," said Wily. "What *is* he trying to hide?"

He climbed down and spotted a computer. This time he didn't need to think twice. He immediately started going through Haruki's photos and emails. In a folder marked "don't delete", he found a video file marked "final agreement". Wily clicked on it and Haruki Horse's face appeared on screen. It was a recording of a video call made the week before.

"So what is your final offer?" said Haruki. His monocle glinted and he spoke with a deep voice.

"One hundred thousand dollars now and another hundred thousand when you finish the task," said the other caller. But it was impossible to work out who it was. The animal wore a cloak that covered its face and its voice had been scrambled by special software.

Haruki flared his nostrils. "And the task is to send Shoma Shrew and Kia Coyote through to the final?"

"That's correct," said the other caller.

Haruki took off his monocle and wiped it slowly with a handkerchief. "I'll think about it," he said.

The other caller was silent for a couple of seconds and then said, "There's nothing to think about. If you refuse, I'll take your sharpest kitchen knife and plunge it straight into your heart."

The call ended and the screen went black.

"Nasty," Wily said to himself.

He copied the file on to his phone and searched the rest of Haruki's desk. In the bottom drawer was a letter from the bank confirming what Charlie had suspected. Haruki was a big spender. Wily also found out that the bank was threatening to make him sell his restaurant.

"OK, I'm coming back up," Wily shouted.

The robot didn't reply.

Wily hurried up the ladder. "Hey, metal-head! Did you hear me?"

He climbed out of the trap door, but the robot was nowhere to be seen. He looked for tracks on the carpet – there was nothing. It was as if the robot had never been in the room.

Wily breathed in. He could smell horse, metal, sushi and then ... rodent. Wily remembered the paw print of the animal that had followed him from the TV studio. That had been a rodent, too. Wily swivelled round.

"Come out, come out, wherever you are," he murmured.

Wily felt a breeze behind him and spun round. Nothing. He moved silently along the corridor and out into the restaurant. The rodent smell was overpowering now. Something lurched out of the darkness. Wily ducked and a pan flew over his head, clattering on to the floor. He turned round and looked at the kitchen doors.

In each of the doors, there was a round window. In one of the windows, there was a face. A face wearing a mask across its muzzle. Wily expected the face to disappear, but it didn't – it stared at him with glittering rodent eyes. The window was at least a metre off the ground. The rodent was clearly very tall or ... could it be ... levitating? A single word immediately leaped into Wily's head.

Ninja.

The face disappeared. Wily clenched his fists. This could be tough. One of his trickiest cases had been the Mystery of the Bald Husky, where he'd had to fight off nineteen ninja chihuahuas. But he'd solved that case and he'd solve this one.

Wily walked towards the kitchen. Suddenly the doors whooshed open and a black streak hurtled through the air, knocking him over. He felt something thumping him on the ear and then everything went black.

WILY FEELS THE HEAT

Wily woke up sweating. Did he have a fever? Then he realized the air around him was hot. He sat up quickly and hit his head on something hard. He threw out his arm and whacked something even harder. There was a small glass window in front of him. Wily peered through and could make out Haruki's kitchen. He was locked inside an oven.

Wily whipped out his phone – no signal. He banged on the door – it didn't budge. The oven was intensely, unbearably hot.

"OK, Wily," he said to himself. "Keep cool."

Wily rooted around in his pockets. His notepad. His false beard. A pair of glasses. And then he put his hand on the gadget that Albert had given him. The small spoon that could transform into any kitchen utensil in the world.

"Steak tenderizer," he said into the microphone at the end.

The spoon whirred and turned into a big metal mallet. Wily whacked the door with it, but it didn't budge – and now he was even hotter.

He tried a potato masher, a spatula and a rolling pin, but he couldn't even dent the door. His tail had started to shrivel and curl up from the heat and his tongue felt like bark.

"If you can't stand the heat," he said to himself, "get out of the kitchen."

An idea dropped into his head. "Toothpick," he said and the gadget whirred into its new shape.

Wily inserted the toothpick carefully into the edge of the oven door, twisting the lock. He heard one catch go *click*, then another. Finally the door popped open and Wily collapsed on to the kitchen floor, gasping. He took a few seconds to cool down, then sprang to his feet.

This was bigger than a cookery competition. Someone wanted him dead.

Wily searched the kitchen for any sign of the ninja. Nothing, except for that same

rodent smell. Then he looked for other clues.
He found a tiny scrap of paper by the kitchen
door. Had it been dropped as the ninja flew at
Wily's head? It had a few numbers scrawled
on it: **14-12-5-13-21-18**. A phone number?
A bank account?

Wily quickly left the restaurant and
ran back to the cave HQ, where a fire was
crackling outside. He told Albert everything
that had happened.

"So you were right," said Albert. "Haruki *was* bribed."

"He used the money to pay off his debts and hire a fleet of robots," said Wily. "Robots don't need wages or lunch breaks or holidays – his money worries are over."

"OK, so do we arrest him?"

"Not yet. Let's make him and the ninja think they've got rid of me," said Wily. "But I want you to stay here and watch Haruki," he continued. "I'm going to talk to Petra Platypus. Whoever bribed Haruki bribed her as well."

Albert sighed. "Be careful, Wily. If that ninja finds you, it'll probably try to kill you again."

"I'm counting on it," said Wily, grinning.

He ran down to the beach and grabbed the turbo surfboard from where he had left it. He jumped on. After the heat of the oven, the ocean spray felt lovely and cool on his fur.

Petra Platypus worked in Sydney. She wrote reviews of cafés and restaurants – usually nasty reviews. Even on the surfboard, it would take Wily a couple of hours to get to Sydney. He had plenty of time to make a phone call.

He rang Sybil Squirrel. Sybil worked for Julius Hound at PSSST. However, unlike Julius, she was happy to share information with Wily and they often ended up cracking cases together.

"Hey, Sybil, sorry to wake you," he said when she answered.

"It's OK," said Sybil. "I'm on the night shift."

"Did Julius mention I ran into him yesterday?"

"Yes, I saw the repair bill from the hotel," said Sybil.

"He said something about investigating a ninja assassin."

"That's right," said Sybil.

"Not a small rodent by any chance?"

Sybil was silent for a couple of seconds. Then she said, "How did you know that?"

"Julius was right for once," said Wily. "I think maybe we're after the same guy."

"The same *girl*," Sybil said. "Rin the Ninja Hamster. Deadliest assassin in the history of the ninja order. But why are *you* after her?"

"I *think* she's involved in fixing a TV cookery competition," said Wily.

"Are you sure?" said Sybil, with a slight laugh. "Sounds a bit … trivial for her."

"I know how it sounds," said Wily.

"But it looks like there might be more to *Megachef* than just cookery."

"OK, MUM," said Sybil. "I'LL SEE YOU AT THE WEEKEND."

"Ah," said Wily. "Did Julius just walk in?"

"THAT'S RIGHT, MUM," said Sybil.

"Can you give me any clues about where Rin might be? Or how to beat her?"

"I KNOW YOU HATE OPERA, MUM," said Sybil, "WE WON'T GO TO THE OPERA. YOU THINK THE SINGING IS LIKE TORTURE."

The line went dead. OK, so Sybil had started talking about opera – that must be the clue. What did the ninja have to do with opera? Was she hiding in an opera house? Wily also thought about the string of numbers again: **14-12-5-13-21-18**. Maybe when he'd spoken to Petra Platypus the clue would make more sense. Wily let out a huge yawn. He tapped a button on the surfboard, putting it on autopilot.

"Should try to get some rest," he murmured.

Two hours later, Wily woke up when
his surfboard bumped against Sydney
Harbour Bridge. He steered the board
towards the shore, leaped off and tucked
it under his arm. Then he crossed the road and
looked up at a large glass building, glinting in
the morning sun. Petra Platypus worked on
the seventh floor, at the *Daily Digest*.

Wily needed a way of sneaking in. If he
announced himself in reception, Petra would
have time to hide or escape or destroy
any evidence. The element of surprise was
important. Wily looked up the side of the
building. He saw a window open on the
seventh floor. This gave him an idea.

He wedged the end of his surfboard into a square of grass on the side of the pavement. One of the security guards had spotted him and was ambling over. *Better move fast*, he thought.

He pulled the top of the surfboard backwards, until it curled back and almost touched the road. It creaked with tension – like it was about to snap. Wily looked up at the seventh-floor window and twisted the board slightly to the left. Then, quick as a flash, he leaped on to it and let go of the end. The board flipped forwards like a diving board, catapulting him through the air.

As he approached the building, Wily straightened his legs. He shot through the seventh-floor window like an arrow, landing in the middle of a busy newspaper office.

A group of young journalist rabbits peered down at him.

"Surf's up," he said, getting to his feet.

Wily strode forwards, looking at the doors
that ran along both sides of the office. On
the last door on the left was the name PETRA
PLATYPUS. He flung it open.

"Haven't you heard of email?" asked Petra.
Her arms were folded and she looked cross.

"I prefer the personal touch," said Wily.

"OK, so who are you?" said Petra. "The manager of the Raw Prawn? The owner of the Itchy Dingo?"

"What makes you think I'm from a restaurant?" asked Wily.

"Oh, come now, don't play that game with me," said Petra. "Every day I write a horrible review of one of the terrible restaurants in this city. People lose their jobs because of what I say. And they always threaten to beat me up or bump me off. As if it's *my* fault their food is disgusting."

"I see," said Wily.

"So let's get this straight," said Petra. "I'm not going to apologize. I just tell the truth."

Petra had moved forwards and was now nose to nose with Wily. Wily's brain was whirring. Petra was clearly as tough as nails. How was he going to make her talk? Then he thought of something. He decided to take a chance.

"The hamster sent me," he said.

There was a split second when Wily thought he'd made a big mistake. But then he saw that it had worked. Petra Platypus was on her knees, gibbering.

"Please, I did what you asked, don't reveal my secret," she stammered.

Wily said nothing.

"I let the shrew and the coyote go through. That was the deal."

"I know," said Wily.

"So what more do you want?"

"A confession," said Wily. He pulled out his phone, pointed it at her and pressed record. "Then you have our word that you will not hear from us again."

Petra looked confused. "You know my secret already."

Wily nodded and said, "But we need to make sure you will not break your word. Confess, and we can trust you."

Petra thought for a second or two. Finally she nodded.

"Ten years ago, I stole ten thousand dollars from my best friend. She was left penniless – she nearly died of hunger. I used

the money to bribe the editor of the *Daily Digest*. He gave me my first job as a food critic. I knew nothing about food then – I know nothing now. My whole career is based on corruption and lies. Five days ago, your hamster friend said she would tell the world the truth unless I agreed to rig the semi-final of *Megachef.* So I did. And I have." Petra stopped talking and looked down at her feet. "Sounds pretty bad when you say it out loud."

For about half a second, Wily felt sorry for Petra. But he still needed to find out who was behind this. And why Rin the Ninja Hamster was involved.

Wily pressed the button on his phone to stop the recording.

"There must be no evidence we have ever spoken," said Wily. "Surrender anything that my hamster friend has ever given you. Any objects. Any letters."

Petra's jaw stiffened.

"Come on," said Wily. "Hand it over."

Petra didn't move.

Wily took another chance. "That includes anything you have *found out*."

It worked. Petra seemed to make a decision. She walked over to her desk and took a piece of paper out of the top drawer.

"Last time the hamster was here, I analyzed the security footage. She climbed on to the roof and then looked at a note in her hand. I zoomed into it. The letters were blurry but, like most newspapers, we have image-sharpening software. It turned the blurry letters into this."

She handed over a piece of paper with four words on it.

RUM ELEVEN NO PEEK

"You're wise to have done that," said Wily.
"We suspected that you had spied on her."

He looked again at the coded message.
What did the four words mean?

At that moment, he felt a light breeze ruffle
the fur on the back of his neck. Then he heard
a scuffling sound. He looked up and sniffed –
that rodent smell again. OK. This time, he'd be
prepared.

"What are you doing?" asked Petra.

Wily picked up a chair and put a finger to
his lips. The hamster was here. But how had
she got here so quickly? And what was her
plan this time? He listened again. The noise
was coming from under the floorboards, then

it seemed to move up to the walls. It was a light, scratchy pattering.

Wily glanced up and at the same time, a black streak crashed through the ceiling. He swung the chair round and pinned the ninja to the wall. She glared at him and snapped a chair leg off with her bare paws, wriggling free. Then they were rolling across the floor, pulling each other's fur and snarling. They burst out of Petra's office and the journalist rabbits all scattered. Wily saw the open window through which he had first entered the building.

"Let's. Take. This. Outside," he grunted.

Wily tore himself away from Rin and ran towards the window. He grabbed a copy of the *Daily Digest*, then leaped out of the window and unfolded the paper. It wasn't the best parachute, but it slowed him down slightly.

He managed to hit the pavement without breaking any bones. Then he glanced over his shoulder.

The ninja was following him.

Good.

Wily grabbed his surfboard, jumped into the harbour and started it up.

He saw Rin dive into a speedboat and throw the owner into the water.

"Time to head out of the city," he muttered to himself.

As Wily powered round the edge of Sydney harbour in the direction of Bondi Beach, the ninja zoomed towards him in her speedboat.

"Let's ride the waves," he said with a smile.

Bondi Beach was famous for its large waves, but today they were dangerously huge.

Wily led the ninja into a massive breaking wave. The wave hit the side of the speedboat, but Rin clung on, still racing after Wily. He led her to a second wave, then a third. Still she stayed on his tail.

Then came the big one. A three-metre-high wave, thundering towards them at top speed.

Perfect, thought Wily. *Time to switch places.*

He headed straight for the wave. Rin seemed to hesitate, but then her eyes flashed with anger and she followed.

Wily rode up the wave, letting it turn his surfboard over. Rin accelerated, hoping to crash right through the wave to the other side. The wave carried Wily over the top of the speedboat. He twisted the board round. Now he was behind Rin. She glanced over her shoulder just as the wave broke. The water pushed her backwards – out of the boat and straight into Wily's arms.

Wily held Rin tightly. She was still dazed from the impact. He rode the wave as it broke, letting the rushing water take them to the shore.

An emu lifeguard rushed over. "What are you two playing at?" he demanded.

"It's OK," said Wily. "The game's over."

RIN FACES THE MUSIC

Wily was on top of the Sydney Opera House. He had set up a small tent, a barbecue and a deck chair. On the barbecue, three sausages were sizzling. Tied to the deck chair was Rin the Ninja Hamster.

"Let me go!" she yelled.

"You can shout all you like," said Wily. "Nobody will hear you up here." He held up a sausage on a fork. "Want one?"

Rin looked at the sausage and her mouth watered.

"Then you'll need to tell me what you're up to," said Wily.

Rin gritted her teeth. "Never," she hissed.

"I know you're not acting alone," said Wily, biting off the end of the sausage. "Someone's paying you. And I've got two clues. The numbers **14-12-5-13-21-18** that you dropped in Haruki's kitchen. And a four-letter code: **RUM ELEVEN NO PEEK**."

Rin smiled and shrugged, as if to say "I don't know what you're talking about".

"You bribed Haruki Horse and Petra Platypus to let the shrew through," said Wily. "But Shoma Shrew hasn't got any money. There's

no way he could have hired you or paid the bribes. So who did? Who's our criminal? Let's see if a little music can help us think."

He opened up a hatch below him that led directly to the opera house. The performers were halfway through a performance and the music floated up.

"A certain squirrel gave me a message about you and opera," smiled Wily. "I think she was telling me that you HATE it."

Rin was gritting her teeth. "Close that hatch," she hissed.

"I can't imagine why," said Wily. "It's so soothing."

"Unbearable," muttered Rin. Her arms were tied, but Wily could see she was desperate to place her hands over her ears.

"Did Kia Coyote hire you?" asked Wily.

The soprano was hitting some high notes.

"Awful – warbling," Rin was mumbling. "Can't – they – just – sing – normally?"

"What about Charlie Cheetah?"

"Can't – concentrate," said Rin. "Terrible – racket."

"Or someone else at the TV studios?" said Wily.

Rin looked at Wily with fury. "Close the hatch! My father used to play this RUBBISH every day when I was trying to study. It's like two fog horns blaring out at each other!"

"So tell me who's behind this."

"Never," said Rin, clenching her jaw.

Wily opened the hatch even wider and tilted the chair over it. Rin was looking straight down at the stage. She was shivering and sweating. "Meaningless – deafening…"

"So tell me which—" Wily began.

"No!" Rin shouted. "You can drop me on to the stage, if you like. I *still* won't tell you which contestant it is."

Wily let the chair fall back and closed the hatch. He smiled at her.

"So it IS one of the contestants," he said.

Rin blinked. "Er, no, I mean, yes." She was angry with herself now.

"That certainly narrows it down," said Wily.

He walked across to his tent and started thinking hard. Shoma, Kia or Lenny? He was certain it wasn't Shoma Shrew or Kia Coyote. And Lenny Lemur had lost, and nobody paid anyone to help them LOSE. Unless…

He felt in his pocket and took out the clues. First the password. He looked at the first five letters. *RUM EL*. That was *LEMUR* backwards. So what happened if he read all of it backwards?

RUM ELEVEN NO PEEK became KEEP ON NEVE LEMUR.

Neve Lemur – not Lenny? Who was Neve?

How about the string of numbers? 14-12-5-13-21-18. Maybe there was a code to crack here, too. What if the numbers became letters? 1 = A, 2 = B, 3 = C, and so on. Then 14-12-5-13-21-18 became N LEMUR!

Wily thought back to the lobby of the Tokyo Lodge Hotel. He remembered seeing Lenny Lemur's mother standing up for her defeated son. Had she been trying to throw everyone off the scent…?

"Lenny's mother wouldn't be called Neve, by any chance?" asked Wily.

"No!" Rin spat back immediately.

"Tut tut," said Wily, shaking his head.

"You should have kept refusing to talk. But *denying* it so strongly. That's as good as a confession."

Wily took out his phone and called Charlie Cheetah.

"Wily," said Charlie through a mouthful of sandwich. "I'm glad you called. You know the show's being filmed tomorrow afternoon. I hope you've got good news."

"What do you know about Lenny Lemur's mother?" asked Wily.

"Nightmare!" replied Charlie. "Threatened to sue me when her son was thrown off the show."

"But she didn't," said Wily.

"No," said Charlie. "In the end, she backed down. Didn't even file a complaint."

"That figures," said Wily. "Listen – do you

know her address?" he asked.

"Lady Neve Lemur, 1 Mongoose Mansion, Kobe," said Charlie.

"OK, gotta go," said Wily.

"Hang on, why—" But Wily had already cut Charlie off and was calling Sybil.

"Sybil," he said. "Thanks for the tip. Your ninja assassin is tied up next to me on top of the Sydney Opera House."

"Course she is," said Sybil.

"Come and get her whenever you're ready," said Wily. "I'm going back to Japan. It's time for the mother of all showdowns."

Back on his surfboard, Wily went through the case in his head. Lenny's mother had paid Rin to scare and bribe the judges. For some reason, she wanted her son to lose. What had

Lenny done to deserve that? He texted Albert, telling him he was off to see his latest suspect. Albert texted back immediately.

OK, GOOD LUCK. I'M WORKING ON A GADGET THAT WILL KNOCK YOU OFF YOUR FEET.

Three hours later Wily was standing outside the Lemur mansion in Kobe. It was early evening. Behind him was an enormous ornamental garden full of fountains, bonsai trees and a large maze. In front was a beautifully carved wooden door. His brain was crackling with ideas. Who should he pretend to be? What disguise should he wear?

Before he had time to knock, the huge bolts slid back. There was a judder as a large handle was turned. Finally there was the shriek of old golden hinges as the door was thrown open. Two footmen were standing on either side of the door and a housekeeper – a trim, humourless chipmunk in a bright white pinafore – glided out.

"Mr Fox," she said. "Do come this way."

Wily blinked. *Interesting*, he thought. Had they known he was coming? He was led down several long corridors and into a gigantic dining room on which a banquet had been laid out. Down one end of the table, he could hear the squeak of a knife and fork on a china plate.

"I thought you might be hungry," said a voice behind a giant fruit bowl. "After all, you've had a busy few days."

Wily stepped forwards and saw Neve Lemur

wearing a large turban and a red cloak. She dabbed her lips with a napkin and gestured at the table full of food.

"Help yourself," she said.

Wily picked up an apple and sniffed it. It seemed safe and, besides, Neve was unlikely to poison her own food.

He took a bite and said, "Why did you do it?"

"The Lemur family owns a string of banks across Japan," said Neve. "My husband died ten years ago and I have had to run the business by myself."

"Must be hard work," said Wily, taking another bite of the apple.

"It is," said Neve. "I have been waiting for Lenny to come of age so he can take over the family business, allowing me to retire."

"I see," said Wily, "but instead he gets into cooking and decides he wants to be a chef."

"Something like that," said Neve.

"So why didn't you just order him to do what you wanted?" said Wily. "I'm sure you can be very persuasive."

"I tried," said Neve. "He resisted. He can be stubborn, you see. He got that from his dunderhead of a father. I realized it would be better if I was openly supportive, while doing everything I could behind the scenes to destroy his dream."

"How did you find Rin?" asked Wily.

"I've used her before," said Neve, "to resolve

other ... business matters."

"Well, sorry to ruin your plans," said Wily, "but I worked out Rin was involved, caught her and have handed her over to PSSST."

"Oh, that's all right," said Neve, blinking her heavy-lidded eyes slowly. "I'm quite capable of handling these matters by myself. For example, you never asked how my husband died."

Wily's teeth clenched. Had he underestimated his enemy?

"You don't want to know?" said Neve. "Well, I'll tell you. Food poisoning."

Wily glanced down at his apple.

"It's the oldest trick in the book," said Neve. "You walk into this room. See me eating. Assume I've been tucking into this food. Whereas, in fact..." Wily could feel his head spinning. "I haven't touched any of it. Because you see..." Wily's vision went blurry.

"It's ALL poisoned."

Uh-oh, Wily thought, *biggest mistake ever.*

He tried to get up, but his legs felt wobbly.
Neve Lemur was watching him with a
triumphant look on her face. Just as he was
about to pass out, he had an idea. He staggered
sideways, tugging one corner of the tablecloth.
As he fell, he pulled the cloth and everything
on it down with him. He heard splattering and
shattering, then everything went quiet.

THE CRAZY MAZE

When Wily woke up, everything was still dark.
His eyes quickly got used to the blackness and
he worked out he was in a kitchen of some
kind. The blinds were down and the lights
were off, but he could make out a sink, an
oven and a cupboard. He appeared to be lying
on a work surface.

"Hello?" he whispered.

A shape on the other side of the kitchen
stood up.

"Thank goodness," it whispered. "I thought

you were a goner."

"Not quite," said Wily.

"I'm amazed you made it," the voice
said. "You had a huge dose of arsenic in
your system. Jolly good job you pulled that
tablecloth off or I'd never have realized
anything was happening."

"Oh, you heard that," Wily said. "Good.
I was hoping it might attract someone's
attention. So who are you?"

"Sorry," muttered the voice. A side lamp
was turned on – it was Lenny Lemur.

"Ah, hello, Lenny," said Wily. "Where am I?"

"You're in my kitchen," said Lenny. "Don't worry, Mother never ventures down here. She always says, 'I can't abide kitchens'. I saw you being carried out of the dining room. Mother thought I was in a business meeting, but it got cancelled so I scooted off early. I watched everything from the landing, where the old girl couldn't see me. I heard Mother giving instructions to the head maid, saying the body should be left in the garage until Aubrey came back. Aubrey's our butler, you see. Anyway, I sneaked down to the garage sharpish and ferried you here. I worked out you'd been poisoned and mixed up an antidote." He pointed to the herb rack behind him. "It seems to have done the trick, thank goodness!"

"Thanks... But why did you help me?" asked Wily.

"Because Mother also said something else

to the head maid," said Lenny. "She said, 'That's the last of this *Megachef* nonsense.'"

"I see," said Wily.

"I also found this in your pocket," said Lenny, holding up a letter from Charlie Cheetah, asking for Wily's help.

"So you put two and two together?" said Wily.

"And came up with 'What the devil is going on?'" said Lenny.

Wily looked at Lenny and breathed in. He tried to pick up any suspicious scents or odours. Was Lenny sweating too much – or too little? Both could suggest he was lying. Wily listened for any shuffling or fidgeting, but Lenny was sitting perfectly still. It seemed he was genuine.

"OK," said Wily, taking a deep breath. He told Lenny everything. Lenny looked upset, then angry, then very angry, then very upset.

"So Mother never really supported my dream of being a chef," he said.

Wily shook his head. "Sorry."

"She wanted me to work in that boring office all day, going to dreary old meetings till the day I died," said Lenny.

Wily nodded. "You got it."

"Well, then there's only one thing for it," said Lenny, punching his right fist into his left paw.

Wily sat up and said, "Now take it easy."

"I've got to leave for Tokyo pronto," said Lenny. "It's the *Megachef* final this afternoon and I'm meant to be on it."

Wily smiled. "Great idea. And I know just how to get you there."

"So where did you leave this flying surfboard thing?" Lenny whispered as they crept along the corridor.

"In a bush in your front garden," said Wily. "Next to a long hedge."

"Ah, by the maze. Then let's go this way." Lenny pushed a bookshelf aside, revealing a secret passage. "This leads straight there."

"Perfect," said Wily. They could still be in Tokyo in time for the show. He ducked into the passage, with a glance over his shoulder. He couldn't see anyone behind them.

Wily followed Lenny as the tunnel twisted and turned. As they reached a long wooden ladder, Wily smelled something. His nose twitched.

"Someone's after us," said Wily. "A marsupial, I think." He sniffed again. "Quite a big one."

"Aubrey," said Lenny. "He's a four-foot wombat. Must have realized you weren't in the garage."

They scrambled through a trap door and found themselves surrounded by hedges.

"We're actually INSIDE the maze," said Wily.

"Don't worry, I know the way out. Unless..." said Lenny.

There was a whirring noise.

"Oh bother," he said, "I was hoping that wouldn't happen."

The hedges around them started to shift.

"It's a mechanical maze," said Lenny. "If you switch it on, every two minutes the hedges change places. Makes it jolly tricky to solve."

Wily watched the hedge in front of him slide across, revealing a new path.

"So we've got two minutes before it changes again," Wily said.

Lenny nodded.

"Let's get started then," Wily said, running on ahead.

Behind him, he heard Aubrey emerging from the trap door – and it sounded like the butler had brought backup.

Wily hit a dead end and then another. He sensed he was on the right path, but then all the hedges started to whir.

"Our two minutes are up," Lenny said, as the maze shifted round and the way ahead was blocked.

"They're over here," growled a voice behind the next hedge.

"OK, first we've got to get rid of your butler," said Wily. "Follow me."

He dived into the hedge in front of them. Lenny looked confused, but dived in, too.

Wily pulled out his kitchen gadget. "Butter knife," he whispered.

"This hedge is on wheels," Wily explained. "We just need to detach it from its rails."

He used the butter knife like a screwdriver and, within a few seconds, it had come free.

"That's frightfully clever," whispered Lenny.

Wily peered through the hedge and saw Aubrey and another wombat ambling towards them. Wily tugged Lenny back out of the hedge.

"Now, on my signal, PUSH," said Wily.

"Righty-ho," said Lenny.

Aubrey looked up and down the path. "Dead end," he snarled, "but look – paw prints."

The hedges around him started to shake.

"Two minutes are up again, sir," said the other wombat.

"NOW," whispered Wily.

As the maze started to shift, Wily pushed the hedge he was in towards Aubrey. Aubrey backed away but Wily kept pushing faster and faster.

"Wh-what's going on?" Aubrey stuttered.

He turned the corner, but Wily and Lenny followed him.

"Turn it off, sir, turn it off," the other wombat gibbered.

Aubrey had taken a remote control out of his pocket and was jabbing at the button. All the other hedges groaned to a halt, but Wily and Lenny kept moving their hedge forwards.

"It's malfunctioning!" Aubrey exclaimed,

as the huge green shape loomed over him.

"Let's get out of here," said the other wombat.

They ran back towards the trap door and jumped inside.

Wily and Lenny stopped pushing and clambered out of the hedge.

"OK," said Wily, panting. "He's gone and the hedges have stopped moving. Now you know the way out, right?"

Lenny smiled and nodded. Within a couple of minutes, they were out of the maze and on the front lawn.

"I left my surfboard behind a bush over there," said Wily. But as they walked across the front lawn, they stopped dead in their tracks.

"Looking for this?" Neve asked. She had five servants with her. One of them, a giant yak, snapped Wily's surfboard in half.

"Looks like you've broken our maze, Lenny," Neve said. "That'll have to come out of your pocket money."

"Mother, I'm twenty-three," said Lenny. "I haven't had pocket money for years."

"Well, that's something we can discuss,"
said Neve. "Let's go back to the house."

"There's nothing to discuss," said Lenny. "You
lied to me, Mother. I'm leaving the business to
become a chef. And you can't stop me!"

Neve sighed. "Very well." She turned to her
servants. "Tie up my son. Kill the fox."

Wily looked at the giant yak and Neve's other
servants. Could he beat them? He wasn't sure.

They moved towards him. Wily adopted a
kung-fu posture.

The yak sneered.

Wily made a few mock swipes at the air with his hands. He practised a few kicks.

The yak lowered his head and prepared to charge.

"This is your last chance to surrender," said Wily, trying to look as fearsome as he could.

The yak was about to sprint forwards when he froze on the spot. Neve and the other servants took three steps backwards. They all had terrified expressions on their faces.

"That's right," yelled Wily. "Fear my fury!"

At the same time, he heard a roaring sound behind him. The servants scattered.

Wily turned slowly and saw one of Haruki's robot waiters floating in mid-air. Albert was perched on its back.

"I brought you a new gadget," said Albert. "Want to try it out?"

THE GRAND FINAL

Five seconds later, Wily, Lenny and Albert
were zooming through the sky, leaving Kobe
far behind them. Wily was under one of the
robot's arms, Lenny was under the other and
Albert was sitting on the robot's back.

"It was quite simple in the end," said
Albert. "I replaced its bottom half with a
rocket fuel tank. Then I installed thrusters
under its wheels and added memory chips
so that it could understand more complex
commands."

"Excellent," said Wily. "And now I must call Charlie."

Charlie picked up the phone immediately. "We're on air in two hours," he hissed. "What's going on?"

"I've got Lenny Lemur with me," said Wily. He briefly explained how Lenny's mother had bribed and blackmailed the judges, aided by Rin the Ninja Hamster.

"I KNEW that shrew's meringue was no good," Charlie huffed. "So now what do I do?"

"Proceed as normal," said Wily. "Tell Haruki and Petra that Rin is captured and their ordeal is over. They can keep their jobs if they judge the final honestly."

"But—"

"In the time available, that's the best option. There's no point punishing them now. I'll be there with Lenny in forty-five minutes."

"What's that whistling noise?" asked Charlie.

"That's the sound of a specially adapted robot waiter hurtling through the air at eight hundred miles per hour with a fox, a mole and a lemur on its back."

"Oh," said Charlie. "OK."

Wily hung up.

They flew north, past Hamamatsu and Mount Fuji.

Twenty minutes later, they touched down in an alley beside the TV studios.

"OK, Lenny, let's get you inside," said Wily. "Albert, you stay here and look out for trouble."

"Trouble?" said Albert, slightly nervously.

"I don't know how Neve will react," said Wily. "She may still try to stop this. Can you patrol the outside of the building with the robot and make sure nobody suspicious gets in?"

Albert nodded. "Come on, matey," he said, tapping a button on the robot's arm.

"SURVEILLANCE MODE," said the robot, and it blasted off into the air with Albert on its back.

Wily and Lenny hurried over to the entrance of the TV studios. The *Megachef* queue was now a lot longer than it had been three days ago. The animals at the front were being ushered in. Several female animals recognized Lenny and screamed in delight.

"It's HIM!"

The security guard said, "Mr Cheetah told me you were coming back, sir. This will make my wife's day, this will."

Lenny couldn't help waving at some of his fans in the queue.

"No time for that," said Wily, pulling him through the door. "The show starts in just over an hour. I need to get you to Charlie Cheetah NOW."

They dashed through the foyer and got into the lift. As they went up, Wily said, "I should probably phone PSSST and have your mother arrested."

Lenny shook his head. "If I win *Megachef*, that will be punishment enough for her. And I WILL win *Megachef*."

The lift doors pinged open and they hurried towards Charlie's office. There was no guard outside today and the door was ajar.

"Strange," said Wily. He was about to step inside when a familiar smell overwhelmed him.

Hamster.

Too late. An arm shot out of the office,

grabbing Lenny by the neck and yanking him inside. Wily dashed after Lenny, but he knew that he couldn't match Rin's speed. He heard a thump and a slam. By the time he was inside the office, Rin was standing behind Charlie's desk. Nobody else appeared to be there.

"Where's Lenny?" snarled Wily.

Rin nodded at a door in the corner of the room. It was Charlie's walk-in fridge. Wily glanced through the window. Inside he saw Lenny, Charlie, Haruki Horse, Petra Platypus, Kia Coyote and Shoma Shrew. They were all shivering and a thin layer of frost had formed on their fur.

"All the stars of *Megachef*," said Rin. "Looks like I put their dreams on ice."

"I left you tied up at the top of the Sydney Opera House," said Wily.

"I remember," said Rin, her eyes narrowing.

"How did you escape from Sybil Squirrel?"

"I didn't," said Rin. "She was pretty tough. But she handed me over to some idiot dog."

"Julius," muttered Wily.

"He put me in a prison car with a nice big window," said Rin. "Easy escape."

"So why are you here?" said Wily. "It's all over. Lenny knows everything – how his mother hired you, what you did to Haruki and Petra…"

"I was hired to stop Lenny winning *Megachef.* And that is what I intend to do."

"Well, I've got a job to finish, too," said Wily.

"Of course you have," said Rin with a half-smile. "That's why we are now going to fight to the death. Ready?" She assumed a fighting pose – arms up like the branches of a tree.

Wily was nervous, but he didn't show it. Rin was younger, faster and stronger than him. He needed to think quickly.

"I'm ready," he said.

He was aware there was a cupboard behind him. As it was Charlie's office, he was pretty sure it would be full of food. He eased it open. Rin sprang through the air towards him at lightning speed. In the same instant, Wily grabbed the first thing he found in the cupboard and flung it at her.

He was in luck. It was a bag of tomatoes. They exploded on Rin's body and face, knocking her off-balance. She rolled back behind the desk, trying to wipe tomato juice out of her eyes. At the same time, she pulled open the desk drawer and threw a jam doughnut at Wily, which whistled past his left ear, splattering on the door.

Wily opened the next cupboard and his paws closed round a bottle of honey. Perfect. He squirted it at Rin. Some hit the floor, but some hit Rin, sticking her fur together and slowing her down. Rin responded with a lump of carrot cake and a custard pudding. They splatted all over Wily's arms and legs.

On the bottom shelf of the cupboard, Wily saw a bag of flour. He grinned, twisted round and flung it straight at Rin.

She dodged and it hit the wall behind her, but it didn't matter.

As the bag exploded, most of the flour settled on her body, turning her white. The rest hissed out across the room, making it look like they were caught in a blizzard.

This limited Rin's movement and vision. Now Wily felt they could fight as equals.

With a handful of squid rings in his fist, he leaped across the room, grabbing Rin's arm. He squashed a squid ring into her ear. Rin stuck a breadstick up Wily's nose, giving it a nasty twist. Wily winced and Rin struggled free.

When he looked up, she was on the ceiling, flicking a button next to one of the fire sprinklers.

Whoosh! Water started pouring down from the ceiling, washing the food off her fur. Wily flung a cake at her, but it disintegrated before it reached her. Within a few seconds, Rin was clean and sleek again.

Time to take this to another level, Wily said to himself, *a much higher level.*

A plan had dropped into his head.

He texted one word to Albert, then grabbed a box of eggs from the cupboard and ran out of the office. He pushed open a door and found himself on a TV set. It looked like they had been filming a western – there was the saloon, the bank and the stables.

Wily could hear Rin whistling through the air behind him. He put the eggs carefully in his pocket. He only had six, so he'd have to use his ammunition carefully. He ran down the TV-set high street and ducked into the saloon, looking for a quick way to get to a higher floor of the studios. But then Rin was in front of him. She jumped forwards, her foot aimed at his jaw. Quick as a flash, Wily threw an egg at her face, which knocked her backwards.

Five eggs left.

While Rin was wiping egg out of her eyes
and ears, Wily ran out of the back of the saloon
and found a lighting rig. He scaled it as quickly
as he could and noticed, in the ceiling, a trap
door leading to the floor above. He opened it
and slipped through. Behind him, he could see
Rin climbing the lighting rig at incredible speed.

Now Wily was on another set. This time, it
looked like they'd been filming a space series.
There was a rocket, a crater and an empty alien
suit. In the corner, he could see scaffolding on
which had been hung a backdrop showing a
spectacular alien sunset. He ran across to it and
started to climb.

But Rin was there in a flash, holding his leg
in an iron grip. Wily threw an egg, then two
more. Rin was still holding on. His fifth egg
finally sent her flying backwards towards the

ground. But almost all his ammunition was gone. He had only one egg left.

Wily sped up, climbing to the top of the scaffolding in a matter of seconds. He saw another ceiling hatch and pulled himself through. He needed to get to the roof.

Wily ran through the next two sets with Rin following close behind. Then he found a door marked "Emergency Staircase". He dived through it and looked up. It led straight to the roof, but there were still five floors to go.

He started to run, but Rin managed to leap in front of him. She pushed Wily down the stairs. As he fell on to his back, he felt hands tight round his neck – he was being strangled. He saw purple splodges in front of his eyes. He couldn't move, he couldn't breathe. He reached into his pocket. Surely the egg had been splattered in the struggle? No, it was cracked, but it was still in one piece. It was his last chance.

Wily dropped the egg through the centre of the stairwell. It plummeted down fifteen floors and splattered on the ground with a loud crack. And just as Wily expected, it echoed.

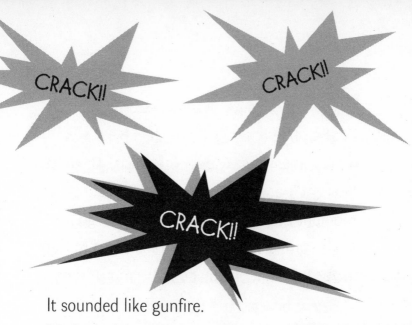

It sounded like gunfire.

Rin looked around anxiously and released her hold. Wily took his chance to get up and dash past her, up the staircase. In the few seconds it took for her to realize what was going on, Wily had a head start. He kept climbing until he reached the door to the roof. He burst through and flung it shut behind him.

Had Albert got his message? Suddenly Rin was back again and he was flattened – she was on top of him, strangling him. What had gone wrong? Wily thought. He was out of eggs and out of ideas. He was beaten, scrambled, fried.

But all at once the air rushed back into Wily's lungs. He looked up and saw Albert and the robot waiter hovering in the air.

"WE RECEIVED YOUR TEXT, SIR," the waiter said. **"THE WORD 'ROOF'. NOW WHERE SHOULD I PUT THIS?"**

The robot had Rin in its left hand. She was lashing out at it, but couldn't make a dent in its hard metal shell.

"Just put her on the top of Mount Fuji for now," said Wily.

"VERY WELL, SIR," said the robot, and shot off into the sky.

"Solving crime in record time," Wily said to himself, and lay back with a smile.

An hour later, Wily was sitting in a café opposite the TV studios, drinking a cup of coffee while *Megachef* blared out on a TV screen in the corner.

Sybil Squirrel was sitting next to him.

"Sorry I'm a bit late," she said. "As soon as I heard how Julius had messed up, I got on a plane to Tokyo."

"It's OK," said Wily. "I handled it."

"So I see. Where have you put her this time?" asked Sybil.

"She's on the top of Mount Fuji, being guarded by a robot waiter," said Wily.

"Naturally," said Sybil. "That makes complete sense."

"I've asked Albert to put a tracking chip on her shoulder," said Wily. "Just in case – you know – Julius lets her escape again."

Sybil smiled. "Good plan."

"And if she does escape, it will trigger opera to be piped into her right ear," said Wily.

"Nice," said Sybil. She glanced up at the TV. "So *Megachef* started on time?"

Wily nodded. "Got everyone out of the fridge with ten minutes to spare. That was enough time to thaw them out."

"Did Shoma Shrew mind dropping out?"

Wily shook his head. "He was petrified of being in the final. He knew his cooking skills weren't up to it. He was delighted when Lenny took his place."

Sybil looked up at the screen again. "Looks like your boy's going to win."

Wily smiled. "Well, he's given up everything to be here."

"He couldn't have done it without you, though," said Sybil.

Wily shrugged. "And I couldn't have done it without you and Albert."

They both sipped their coffee.

"You know you have a blob of jam dangling from your nose, don't you?" said Sybil.

"Of course," said Wily, brushing it off.

"And a lump of cheese in your ear," Sybil added.

"All deliberate," said Wily, removing it.

"In fact, you could start a restaurant with all the food in your fur," said Sybil, looking him up and down.

Wily shuddered. "No cooking. No restaurants. The only thing I'm hungry for is my next case."

His phone started to buzz. He didn't recognize the number.

"And here it is," he said, lifting the phone to his ear. He winked at Sybil. "My mouth's watering already."